THIS STARFISH BAY BOOK BELONGS TO

....

THE LAST LEOPARD

Starfish Bay® Children's Books
An imprint of Starfish Bay Publishing
www.starfishbaypublishing.com

THE LAST LEOPARD

ISBN 978-1-76036-088-7
First Published 2019
Printed in China by Toppan Leefung Printing Limited
20th Floor, 169 Electric Road, North Point, Hong Kong

Originally published as “最后一只豹子” in Chinese
English translation rights from Tomorrow Publishing House

Thank you to Courtney Chow, Marlo Garnsworthy and Na Zhou (in alphabetical order) who were involved in translating and editing this book.

Our thanks also go out to Elyse Williams for her creative efforts in preparing this edition for publication.

THE LAST LEOPARD

Written by Wenxuan CAO
Illustrated by Rong LI

In the wilderness, a leopard was looking for other leopards.
He had searched for several days, but he had found not a single leopard.
"I might be the last leopard left in the world," he thought.

Yet, undeterred, he persisted with his search.
The wilderness was vast and boundless.

Although he was thirsty, he drank only on rainy days.

One day, he saw a wild pigeon flying in the sky.
Seeing the leopard, the wild pigeon excitedly
landed before him.

Just as the leopard was about to ask if the pigeon had seen other leopards, the wild pigeon said, “Have you ever seen other wild pigeons?”

The leopard shook his head. "I'm very sorry, I haven't seen wild pigeons in a long, long time."
The wild pigeon sadly wondered, "Am I the only wild pigeon left in the world?"
The leopard hastily comforted the wild pigeon. "No, keep on searching." He asked, "Have you ever seen other leopards?"

"I'm very sorry," said the wild pigeon. "I haven't seen another leopard in a long, long time."

The leopard sadly asked, "Am I the only leopard left in the world?"

The wild pigeon comforted the leopard in return. "No, keep on searching. Bye! Good luck!" And with that, the wild pigeon flew into the sky.

"Bye! Good luck to you, too!" The leopard continued his search.

Feeling quite tired, the leopard
fell asleep beside a rock.

He was awakened by a squeak. Opening his eyes, he saw a groundhog jumping here and there.

The leopard stood up. “Have you ever seen other leopards?” he asked.
“I’m very sorry,” said the groundhog. “I haven’t seen leopards in a long, long time.”
The leopard sadly pondered, “Am I the only leopard left in the world?”
The groundhog seemed very curious. “Must you see other leopards?”
“Of course!” said the leopard. “Don’t you want to see other groundhogs?”
The groundhog looked surprised. “Am I not the only groundhog in the world?”
To the groundhog’s seeming astonishment, the leopard asked, “Don’t you know you’re not the only groundhog in the world?”
The groundhog said, “For as long as I can remember, I’ve never thought there would be a second groundhog.”

The leopard sighed. "Perhaps, long before you were old enough to remember things, all the other groundhogs had already disappeared."
He glanced at the groundhog with sympathy, sighed once more, and continued searching.

In the wilderness, the leopard kept walking and walking...
And one day, he saw a big tree. He hadn't seen a tree in a long, long time.

It was an oak tree.
The leopard ran to it.

He lay down in the pleasant shade, which
he hadn't enjoyed in a long, long time.

All of a sudden, the oak tree began to talk. "Have you ever seen other oak trees?" The leopard was taken aback and stood up. He looked up at the oak tree and shook his head. "I'm very sorry, I haven't seen an oak tree in a long, long time."
The oak tree said sadly, "Am I the only oak tree left in the world?"
The leopard comforted the oak. "No, maybe tomorrow I'll see another oak tree. Have you ever seen other leopards?"

"I'm sorry to say I haven't seen any leopards in a long, long time," said the oak tree.

The leopard felt discouraged and weak. He sagged wearily under the oak tree for a long time, until he regained his spirit. He firmly told the tree, "I will certainly meet another oak tree!"

The oak tree nodded. "If you do, just tell it another oak tree is here!"

The leopard continued walking...
It finally rained! While running, he reared his head and drank the rain until his thirst was eventually quenched.

The rain stopped.
In front of him appeared a pond in which
the clouds of the sky drifted.
He ran toward it. It had been so long since
he had seen a pond.

Upon arriving, he was shocked by what he saw. There was a leopard in the water! He looked at the other leopard in astonishment. The leopard in the water stared back in astonishment.

What a handsome leopard it was!

Watching the other leopard, he suddenly felt a little ashamed. The other leopard looked back with the same expression.
He extended his forepaw to touch the leopard in the water, and the leopard in the water raised his forepaw.

He lay down by the pond, staring at the
leopard in the water.
The sun beat down on the leopard. It was like a
burning fireball in the sky.
The leopard in the water gradually faded. The
leopard rubbed his eyes and composed himself, but
still he saw nothing in the water.

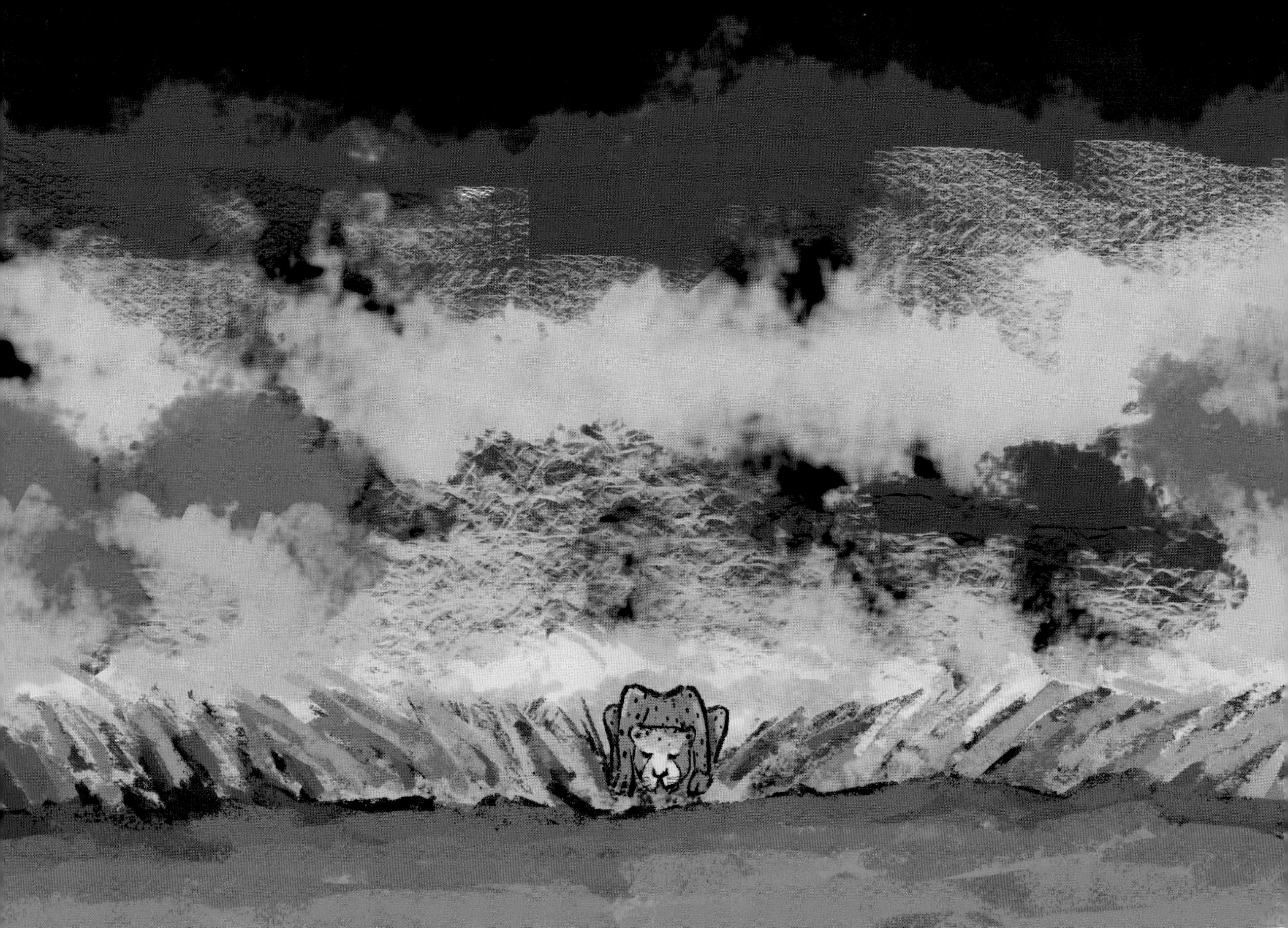

He continued to lie beside the pond.
He would patiently wait for the leopard
to return. He was sure the other leopard
would come back.

After a while, his eyes felt heavy, and
eventually he closed them.
It began to rain again, and the pond filled
rapidly with water.

The rain stopped, and the sky cleared. Beside the pond, the leopard lay motionless. In the water, there was also a leopard, absolutely motionless. The other leopard had returned. But the leopard would never be able to see the leopard in the water, for he had fallen asleep forever.

THE AUTHOR

Wenxuan Cao was born in 1954 in Yancheng, Jiangsu, China, and is a professor of Chinese literature at Peking University. As one of China's most esteemed children's books writers, he has published dozens of works and won more than 40 awards. His work has been translated into English, French, German, Japanese, Korean, and more. In 2016, he became the first Chinese author to receive the Hans Christian Andersen Award. His works express his concern for the lifestyle and emotional well-being of children and adolescents.

THE ILLUSTRATOR

Rong Li, born in 1980 in Shanghai, grew up in Nanjing, China. While studying, she also worked. She enjoys writing, drawing, and creating animations. Currently residing in Beijing, she runs a children's publishing house.